Carlos & Carmen

The Green Surprise

by Kirsten McDonald
illustrated by Erika Meza

Calico Kid

An Imprint of Magic Wagon
abdopublishing.com

For my two sisters—who always make room for me in their tents —KKM

To my two Carlos, and specially both of my parents; who taught me to value changes, movings, carnes asadas, mischiefs, surprises and the beautiful moments you can only live with your family. Gracias: ilos quiero! —EM

abdopublishing.com

Printed in the United States of America, North Mankato, Minnesota.
102015
012016

THIS BOOK CONTAINS
RECYCLED MATERIALS

Written by Kirsten McDonald
Illustrated by Erika Meza
Edited by Heidi M.D. Elston
Designed by Candice Keimig

Library of Congress Cataloging-in-Publication Data

McDonald, Kirsten, author.
  The green surprise / by Kirsten McDonald ; illustrated by Erika Meza.
    pages cm. -- (Carlos & Carmen)
  Summary: For twins Carlos and Carmen, Uncle Alex's big green surprise turns into the best backyard camping experience ever.
  ISBN 978-1-62402-138-1
1. Backyard camping--Juvenile fiction. 2. Hispanic American families--Juvenile fiction. 3. Uncles--Juvenile fiction. 4. Twins--Juvenile fiction. 5. Brothers and sisters--Juvenile fiction. [1. Camping--Fiction. 2. Hispanic Americans--Fiction. 3. Family life--Fiction. 4. Uncles--Fiction. 5. Twins--Fiction. 6. Brothers and sisters--Fiction.] I. Meza, Erika, illustrator. II. Title.
  PZ7.1.M4344Gr 2016
  [E]--dc23
                                                    2015026229

Table of Contents

Chapter 1
Hoorays!

On Saturday afternoon, the Garcia family was in the backyard. Carlos and Carmen were playing soccer.

Mamá was scratching Spooky, their cat. Papá was getting the grill ready.

Papá called to the twins, "Your favorite uncle, Tío Alex, is coming today."

Carlos and Carmen stopped kicking the ball and ran to the deck.

"Tío Alex is coming?" asked Carmen.

"He's coming today?" added Carlos.

"Yes to both of you," laughed Papá.

Then Carlos and Carmen jumped up and down and shouted, "Hooray!"

Papá added with a wink, "He's bringing a fun sorpresa. A big, green sorpresa."

"A surprise?" asked Carlos.

"Double hooray!" shouted Carmen.

"And, también," Mamá said with a laugh, "he's spending the night."

Carlos and Carmen froze. Their eyes got big. Their smiles got bigger.

"It's triple hooray if he's spending the night!" shouted Carlos.

"No!" laughed Carmen, shaking her head at her twin. "Tío Alex spending the night has to be at least a four-iple hooray!"

Chapter 2
Lumpy Green Surprise

An hour later, Tío Alex drove up in his blue car.

"Tío Alex! Tío Alex!" the twins shouted as they ran to greet him.

The twins leaned in his car window.
They looked everywhere inside the car.
"Where is it?" demanded Carmen.
"Where is the surprise?" said Carlos.
Tío Alex laughed. "Ya basta, you
two! Let me get out of my car."
The twins followed Tío Alex to the
back of his car. Inside the trunk was a
lumpy green bag.

"That doesn't look like a very fun surprise," said Carmen sadly.

"Oh, no?" laughed Tío Alex. "Just wait."

Tío Alex carried the lumpy green bag to the backyard. He opened it and shook everything out.

Carlos and Carmen saw long silver poles. They saw short yellow stakes. They saw a big green blob.

"Come help," called Tío Alex.

The twins helped unfold the big green blob. They helped put yellow stakes in loops along the edges of the blob. They helped push the stakes into the ground.

It was starting to get exciting. It was starting to feel like a surprise.

Mamá helped Tío Alex put the poles together. Then, as if by magic, the big green blob became a big green tent!

"Can we go inside?" asked Carmen.

"What would you two think about having a camp-out?" asked Tío Alex.

"A camp-out?" asked Carlos.

"Here in our backyard?" added Carmen.

"Yes, a camp-out here in your backyard," said Mamá, laughing.

"In the big green tent?" asked Carlos.

"Yes, in the big green tent," added Tío Alex.

"This is the best surprise ever!" squealed Carmen, and she jumped into Tío Alex's arms.

"I think this is now a five-iple hooray sorpresa!" added Carlos, jumping onto Tío Alex's back.

Then with the twins hugging him tightly, Tío Alex spun around and around and around.

Chapter 3
Ready

The Garcia family set up their picnic supper. Carmen brought a bowl of salad. Carlos brought a basket of corn chips.

19

Mamá brought bowls of red salsa and green salsa. And Tío Alex brought a plate of watermelon slices.

Papá finished grilling the meat and announced, "The carne asada and tortillas are ready. Let's eat!"

They ate tortillas wrapped around slices of grilled steak. They ate salad and chips and salsa. They ate juicy slices of watermelon.

"Can we get our sleeping bags yet?" asked Carmen.

"¡Dios mío! You two can hardly sit still," said Papá.

"It's getting dark," said Tío Alex. "I have two more little sorpresas for you." He pulled two small flashlights from his back pockets and handed one to each twin.

"Thanks!" shouted the twins.

Chapter 4
Camping Out

Carlos and Carmen wriggled down into their sleeping bags. They made swirls of light on the tent walls with their new flashlights.

They told funny stories, and they sang silly songs.

"Are you sleepy?" asked Carlos.

"A little," answered Carmen with a yawn.

The twins got quiet. They listened to the music playing softly in their house. They listened to the crickets chirping in the grass. They listened to something brushing against the door of the tent.

"¿Qué es?" asked Carmen.

"Do you think it's a monster?" asked Carlos.

Just then the twins heard a soft *murr-uhhh.*

Carmen laughed. "I know that monster."

She unzipped the tent door and let Spooky, the cat, inside.

The twins settled back into their sleeping bags with Spooky nestled between them.

They still heard the music. They still heard the crickets. But now they heard footsteps that were getting closer and closer.

"Do you think that's a monster?" Carlos whispered.

Before Carmen could answer, the tent door started unzipping. Tío Alex poked his head in.

"Got room for uno más?" he asked.

Carlos and Carmen giggled. And, Carlos made a spot for Tío Alex.

The four of them lay side by side in the tent. They heard the music, and they heard the crickets. They also heard another set of footsteps that was getting closer and closer.

The tent door unzipped again. This time, Papá crawled into the tent.

"Make room for me, Carmencita," he said as he stretched out next to her.

Now the five of them lay side by side in the tent. They could all hear the music and the crickets.

They could all hear doors in the house opening and closing and opening and closing. Then they heard another set of footsteps that got closer and closer.

"I think I know who that is," said Carlos with a laugh.

"Me too," giggled Carmen.

Mamá pushed her way into the tent with a laundry basket filled with blankets and pillows.

Then Mamá, Papá, and Tío Alex snuggled into blankets next to Carlos and Carmen and Spooky. It was the perfect big green sorpresa.

Spanish to English

carne asada – grilled meat

¡Dios mío! – Goodness gracious!

Mamá – Mommy

Papá – Daddy

¿Qué es? – What is it?

sorpresa – surprise

también – also

Tío – Uncle

uno más – one more

ya basta – that's enough